Dear Parent:
Your child's love of reading starts here!

Every child learns to read in a different way and at his or her own speed. Some go back and forth between reading levels and read favorite books again and again. Others read through each level in order. You can help your young reader improve and become more confident by encouraging his or her own interests and abilities. From books your child reads with you to the first books he or she reads alone, there are I Can Read Books for every stage of reading:

SHARED READING
Basic language, word repetition, and whimsical illustrations, ideal for sharing with your emergent reader

BEGINNING READING
Short sentences, familiar words, and simple concepts for children eager to read on their own

READING WITH HELP
Engaging stories, longer sentences, and language play for developing readers

READING ALONE
Complex plots, challenging vocabulary, and high-interest topics for the independent reader

ADVANCED READING
Short paragraphs, chapters, and exciting themes for the perfect bridge to chapter books

I Can Read Books have introduced children to the joy of reading since 1957. Featuring award-winning authors and illustrators and a fabulous cast of beloved characters, I Can Read Books set the standard for beginning readers.

A lifetime of discovery begins with the magical words **"I Can Read!"**

Visit www.icanread.com for information
on enriching your child's reading experience.

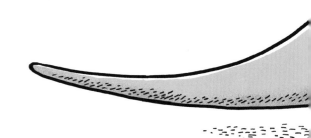

I Can Read Book® is a trademark of HarperCollins Publishers.

Danny and the Dinosaur: The Big Sneeze
Copyright © 2018 by Anti-Defamation League Foundation, The Authors Guild Foundation, ORT America, Inc., United Negro College Fund, Inc.
All rights reserved. Manufactured in China.
No part of this book may be used or reproduced in any manner whatsoever without written permission except in the case of brief quotations embodied in critical articles and reviews. For information address HarperCollins Children's Books, a division of HarperCollins Publishers, 195 Broadway, New York, NY 10007.
www.icanread.com

Library of Congress Control Number: 2018934062
ISBN 978-0-06-241053-5 (trade bdg.)—ISBN 978-0-06-241052-8 (pbk.)

Book design by Celeste Knudsen
18 19 20 21 22 SCP 10 9 8 7 6 5 4 3 2 1 ❖ First Edition

I Can Read!

BEGINNING 1 READING

Syd Hoff's

DANNY AND THE DINOSAUR

The Big Sneeze

Written by Bruce Hale

Illustrated in the style of Syd Hoff by Charles Grosvenor

Colors by David Cutting

HARPER

An Imprint of HarperCollinsPublishers

It was a rainy day, but a fun day.

Danny and the dinosaur got drenched.

But the next day, Danny woke up
with a sore throat and sniffles.

And the dinosaur had

a little cough!

"You're staying in bed, buddy,"

said Danny's father.

"And I'm taking care of you,"

said his mother.

"But I'm not that sick, Mom,"

said Danny.

"Better safe than sorry," she said.

At the museum, the director
told the dinosaur,
"You need to take a day off."

"But I'm not that sick,"

said the dinosaur.

"Get some rest," said the director.

11

Danny's mother covered him

in lots of blankets

to keep him warm and cozy.

The museum director did his best
to make the dinosaur comfortable.

Danny's mother brought him
chicken soup for his sore throat.

The director brought the dinosaur

some water for his cough.

The day seemed longer
than forever.
There was nothing to do
but lie in bed.

Danny and the dinosaur
felt bored.

Danny phoned the dinosaur.

"Sorry I can't play today.

I'm sick in bed."

"Me too," said the dinosaur.

"Being sick is no fun.

Feel better soon!"

Danny's mom brought out

his old jigsaw puzzle.

The director let the dinosaur
play with a jigsaw puzzle too.

Danny's mother played cards
with him to pass the time.

At the museum, the dinosaur

tried playing rock-paper-scissors,

but the cavemen were no fun.

Danny sneezed.

Achoo! Achoo! Achoo!

His mom brought him tissues.

But when the dinosaur sneezed . . .

ACHOOOO!

26

Everybody ran and hid.

At the end of the day,

Danny and the dinosaur

each curled up in their own beds

with a good book

and got plenty of rest.

The next morning,

Danny and the dinosaur

woke up feeling much better.

They were well enough to go outside.

"How was your sick day?"
Danny asked.

"Not bad," said the dinosaur.

"But nothing beats feeling better,"
said the dinosaur.

"Except maybe spending time with
your best buddy," said Danny.